BEYOND THE DENTAL CHAIR

A Journey from Dentist to Hospital Admin

Dr Salil Choudhary

Copyright © <2025> <Dr Salil Choudhary>

Made with ♥ on the Notion Press Platform

www.notionpress.com

This book is dedicated to all those hard-working hospital administrators who left clinical practice to make hospitals a better place to work

Preface

This story began with a question.

What happens when someone trained to treat individual patients begins to see cracks in the system that treats them all?

In the corridors of hospitals, amid the beeping monitors and shuffling of paper files, there are stories that go unnoticed—not because they lack drama, but because they lack visibility. This narrative was born out of one such story. A tale of quiet revolution, of listening more than speaking, of designing instead of diagnosing.

Aarav Mehta's journey is fictional, but his challenges are real. Across the world, healthcare professionals are waking up to the realization that healing is not just clinical—it is also logistical, operational, human. It is about designing systems that breathe with compassion and function with precision.

This book is for every intern who feels like an outsider for asking too many questions. For every doctor who sees patients suffer not for lack of treatment, but for lack of process. And for every administrator who still believes that spreadsheets and structure can, indeed, save lives.

May this story inspire you to look at hospitals differently—not just as buildings where healing happens, but as living systems that must be cared for, just like the people they serve.

— Dr Salil Choudhary

Acknowledgments

No story, especially one rooted in transformation, is written alone.

To my parents—thank you for instilling in me the value of hard work and integrity. Your unwavering support, even when the path I chose looked unfamiliar, gave me the strength to pursue it with confidence.

To my wife, Dr.Saloni—your belief in me, your quiet strength, and your companionship have been my anchor through every late night, every draft, and every doubt. Your insights and love are woven into the very fabric of this work.

To my daughter, Anvesha—though young, you are the light that reminds me daily why healing systems matter. May you grow up in a world where hospitals are safe, kind, and ready—for everyone.

And to my mentor, Dr. Mudit Saxena—thank you for opening the doors of healthcare administration for me. Your mentorship changed the course of my life, and this book would not exist without your early encouragement and continued guidance.

This book is a tribute to each of you.

With Deepest Gratitude

Dr Salil Choudhary

Prologue: The Unseen Corridor

Hospitals are full of corridors—some leading to operating theatres, some to recovery wards, others to quiet corners where loved ones sit holding hope in trembling hands. But the most important corridors are the unseen ones—the ones that connect intention to execution, empathy to systems, healing to design.

Aarav Mehta had never set out to find those corridors. He had entered his internship year with the same hopes most dental students carry—gain clinical expertise, sharpen skills, perhaps set up a private practice someday. His hands were steady, his instincts sharp. But something inside him stirred every time he saw a disorganized emergency queue, a misfiled patient chart, or a nurse stretched too thin between duties.

It wasn't dissatisfaction. It was discomfort—an ache that said, *"There must be a better way."*

This story isn't about a young man abandoning his profession. It's about a young man expanding its definition. It's about fire and files, resistance and resolve, friends lost and faith found. It's about what happens when a dentist dares to trade his chair for a corridor, his tools for a whiteboard—and discovers that the heart of healthcare doesn't just beat in stethoscopes.

It beats in systems.

And sometimes, the boldest form of healing… is redesign.

1. The Reluctant Healer

Aarav Mehta stood before the dental chair, adjusting his gloves as his patient, a middle-aged man with a swollen jaw, winced in pain. The hospital's dental OPD buzzed with activity—nurses moving between stations, sterilizers humming in the background, and the muffled voices of senior doctors giving instructions.

"You're good at this, Aarav," Dr. Deshmukh, his supervisor, said, observing his gentle yet precise extraction technique. "Ever considered oral surgery?"

Aarav forced a smile. He had always been good with his hands, his practical work earning him top grades. Yet, his heart wasn't in it. He found himself more drawn to the administrative side of the hospital—the smooth orchestration of patient flow, the management of resources, and the strategy behind running a healthcare institution.

Later that evening, while filling out patient reports at the duty desk, he overheard a conversation between the hospital's administrative head and the director.

"We need better coordination between departments. The patient turnover is high, but efficiency is dropping," the administrator said.

Aarav's ears perked up. He knew exactly what they were talking about. He had observed inefficiencies firsthand—overbooked appointments, mismanaged patient records, delays in sterilization. His mind started forming solutions, strategies to improve workflows.

That night, as he sat in his small apartment, the weight of his dilemma pressed down on him. His parents had sacrificed so much to get him through dental school. His mother often reminded him of the years of tuition fees and the dreams they had of him running his own clinic one day. How could he tell them that the thought of spending a lifetime fixing teeth no longer excited him?

The next morning at breakfast, he decided to broach the topic with his parents.

"Maa, Baba, I've been thinking…" he began hesitantly.

His father, Dr. Vinod Mehta, a seasoned dentist, looked up from his newspaper. "Thinking about what, beta?"

Aarav took a deep breath. "About my career. I know I'm good at clinical work, but I've been drawn towards the management side of hospitals. The way the system runs, the way decisions impact patient care on a larger scale— it interests me more than individual treatments."

There was silence. His mother's face fell, and his father's expression hardened.

"So, you want to throw away your education?" his father asked, his voice laced with disappointment.

"No, Baba. I want to use my education differently. I believe I can make a bigger impact if I work on hospital administration."

His mother shook her head. "But you're a doctor, Aarav. You have a gift. Why would you want to waste it behind a desk?"

Aarav clenched his jaw. He had anticipated resistance, but the outright dismissal stung. "It's not wasting my skills, Maa. It's using them in a different way. Someone has to ensure that hospitals run efficiently, that patients get the best care possible, that doctors aren't overworked."

His father sighed. "You've always been practical, Aarav. But don't confuse curiosity with passion. Clinical practice is your real skill. You'll regret it if you walk away from it."

Aarav swallowed hard. He wasn't expecting immediate acceptance, but he had hoped for understanding. "I just want you to consider that there's more to healthcare than just treating patients."

His mother placed a gentle hand on his. "Think it over properly, beta. You've worked too hard to throw this away."

As he left for the hospital that day, the weight of their words sat heavy on his shoulders. He knew this wouldn't be easy, but deep down, he also knew that his future lay beyond the dental chair.

2. The Hidden Path

The next few days were a whirlwind of emotions for Aarav. He felt torn between what he was trained to do and what he truly wanted to pursue. Every extraction, every root canal, and every patient consultation left him feeling unfulfilled. His hands worked mechanically, but his mind constantly wandered to the larger workings of the hospital.

The idea of stepping away from clinical practice gnawed at him. He had spent years mastering the art of dentistry—how could he justify leaving it behind? And yet, the moments he spent observing hospital management intrigued him in a way he hadn't felt in a long time.

During lunch breaks, instead of joining his fellow interns in the cafeteria, he found himself drawn to the administrative wing. He would stand near the records department, watching how patient files were transferred, how appointment schedules were managed, and how emergency cases were prioritized. The inefficiencies were glaring. Paper records got misplaced, communication between departments was slow, and staff often seemed overworked and under-supported.

One evening, he stayed late at the hospital, unable to shake off his thoughts. As he wandered through the dimly lit corridors, he found himself outside the operations control room. Inside, a woman in a crisp blue saree and a name badge that read 'Dr. Aditi Nair – Chief Operating Officer' was engaged in a serious discussion with a few administrators.

Curious, Aarav hesitated before knocking lightly on the glass door. Dr. Nair turned, her sharp eyes studying him before she nodded. "Yes?"

"Dr. Nair, I'm Dr. Aarav Mehta, an intern in the dental department," he introduced himself, suddenly feeling self-conscious. "I… I've been observing how things work here, and I think there are areas that could be improved. I was wondering if I could learn more about hospital administration."

Dr. Nair raised an eyebrow but gestured for him to enter. "You're a dentist, Dr. Mehta. Why the sudden interest in management?"

Aarav hesitated, then decided to be honest. "I enjoy clinical work, but I feel like my skills could be used to improve how the hospital functions overall. I've noticed inefficiencies in patient flow, record management, and scheduling. I think these issues impact patient care just as much as medical treatment does."

Dr. Nair leaned back in her chair, a hint of amusement in her expression. "Most doctors don't pay attention to these things. They see patients and go home. What makes you different?"

Aarav swallowed. "I don't know. I just… can't ignore it. I feel like if we optimize processes, we could make a real difference in how the hospital runs."

She studied him for a moment before speaking. "Hospital administration isn't just about fixing broken systems, Dr. Mehta. It's about leadership, crisis management, and balancing medical expertise with operational efficiency. If you truly want to understand this world, you'll need to see it firsthand."

Aarav nodded eagerly. "I want to learn."

Dr. Nair smiled slightly. "Alright. Be in the ER tomorrow morning at seven. If you're serious about this, you'll start by understanding how emergency cases are handled. That's where hospital management is tested the most."

Aarav felt a rush of excitement. "I'll be there."

As he left the office, he felt a strange mix of relief and anticipation. For the first time in weeks, he felt like he was taking a step in the right direction. He still didn't know how to balance this with his clinical duties, but for now, he had found a mentor who might help him navigate this uncharted path of hospital administration. Now he just wanted to get started.

3. Dr. Aditi Nair – The Architect of Order

Dr. Aditi Nair had always been a force of nature, known for her sharp intellect and relentless pursuit of efficiency. Raised in a family of doctors, she had initially followed the expected path into clinical medicine. But unlike her peers, she had an innate curiosity about the systems that governed hospitals. Why did some hospitals run like well-oiled machines while others struggled with constant chaos?

After completing her MBBS, she practiced as a physician for a few years, but she quickly realized that individual patient care, while fulfilling, wasn't enough. She saw how administrative failures often led to preventable errors, miscommunication, and unnecessary delays in treatment. Determined to make a larger impact, she pursued an MBA in Hospital Administration, a decision that baffled many of her colleagues.

Her rise in the field was meteoric. She joined a private hospital as a junior administrator and, within a few years, became the youngest Chief Operating Officer in the institution's history. Under her leadership, patient satisfaction scores improved, hospital readmission rates dropped, and financial efficiency skyrocketed. Her methods were unconventional—she introduced digital tracking systems for patient records, streamlined interdepartmental coordination, and even initiated leadership training for senior doctors to foster better teamwork.

At her current hospital, she was both respected and feared. She had a no-nonsense approach, and while some found her intimidating, no one could deny her results. She had an open-door policy, but only those genuinely interested in hospital management ever dared to enter.

So, when Aarav knocked on her office door that evening, she immediately recognized something different in his eyes. Unlike most interns, he wasn't there to complain about policies—he was there to understand them. And that, in her experience, was the mark of someone who had the potential to truly change the system.

"You want to learn about hospital administration?" she asked, scanning him carefully.

"Yes," Aarav replied firmly. "I believe I can make a real difference here."

Dr. Nair leaned forward. "Good. Because hospital administration is not just about paperwork, Dr. Mehta. It's about crisis management, about understanding how policies affect real people, and about ensuring that medical staff can do their jobs without unnecessary hindrances."

Aarav nodded, his admiration growing.

"Tomorrow," she continued, "you'll shadow me. You'll see what goes into keeping this hospital running. If you can handle it, maybe you do belong in this world."

For the first time in weeks, Aarav felt a sense of direction. He wasn't just an intern torn between two paths—he was now a student of a new discipline, one that held the key to the change he wanted to make

4. Walking the Line

Aarav's days became a balancing act between clinical duties and administrative shadowing. Mornings were spent in the OPD, attending to patients, while afternoons saw him observing how different hospital departments functioned. He quickly realized that running a hospital was a delicate dance between efficiency and chaos.

One day, while in the middle of a complex root canal procedure, he received an urgent message from Dr. Aditi Nair. "Mass casualty incident in the ER. Come now if you want to understand real-time hospital management."

His heart pounded. This was exactly the kind of situation he wanted to learn from, but he was in the middle of a procedure. He glanced at his patient, then at the junior resident assisting him.

"Dr. Sharma, can you take over?" he asked hesitantly.

The resident frowned but nodded. "Go, but don't make a habit of this."

Aarav rushed to the ER. The scene was chaotic, patients on stretchers, doctors shouting orders, nurses scrambling for supplies. Dr. Nair stood in the centre, directing the flow of treatment and bed allocation. He saw her make snap decisions about which patients needed immediate surgery and which could wait.

She turned to him. "This is hospital administration in action. Not just papers, but real-time crisis management. Watch and learn."

For the next two hours, Aarav observed the structured chaos. He helped where he could—fetching supplies, checking patient statuses—but mostly, he absorbed how crucial decision-making worked at a high level.

When he returned to the OPD, the patient he had left was gone. Dr. Deshmukh was waiting for him.

"You left a procedure halfway for admin work?" he asked, voice cold. "You're a doctor first, Aarav."

Aarav looked down, guilt creeping in. "I… I had to see how the hospital functioned during emergencies."

Dr. Deshmukh sighed. "I won't stop you from exploring administration, but you need to remember—if you lose credibility as a doctor, no one in this hospital will respect you as an administrator."

Aarav nodded, understanding the weight of the words. He needed to find a balance, but deep down, he knew that what he had witnessed in the ER only strengthened his resolve. Hospital management wasn't just paperwork—it was about making decisions that saved lives.

And that, he realized, was exactly where he wanted to be.

5. Straddling Two Worlds

Aarav struggled to balance his dual responsibilities. He continued treating patients during the day while shadowing Dr. Nair in the evenings. His clinical supervisors noticed his divided focus, and whispers began circulating among the interns. Some admired his ambition, while others resented his shift in priorities. Despite the murmurs, Aarav remained steadfast, knowing that his vision extended beyond the chair.

One afternoon, during his routine rounds, he was assigned to assist in the NICU—a place where fragile newborns clung to life, and every second mattered. The air carried a mixture of antiseptic, baby powder, and the quiet hum of incubators keeping the premature infants warm. As he checked the vitals of a newborn, he noticed something odd—the lights flickered for a second and then stabilized. It was subtle, but enough to make him uneasy.

Following his instincts, Aarav stepped toward the main electrical panel in the NICU. He examined it closely and noticed irregular sparking. Frowning, he tapped the panel lightly, and a tiny arc of electricity snapped between two loose wires before disappearing. His heart skipped a beat. This wasn't just an occasional flicker—it was a potential fire hazard in the most sensitive ward of the hospital.

His first reaction was to inform the NICU nursing supervisor. "Ma'am, I think there's an issue with the electric panel," he said, pointing at the sparks.

The supervisor, already overwhelmed with patient care, barely spared him a glance. "We've had minor flickers before. Maintenance checks it regularly. Don't worry, doctor."

Aarav wasn't convinced. He immediately reported the issue to the hospital's maintenance head, Mr. Sharma.

"Sir, I was in the NICU, and I saw irregular sparking in the main panel. This could be dangerous. We need to get it checked immediately."

Mr. Sharma, a man in his late fifties with years of experience, waved him off. "Dr. Aarav, I appreciate your concern, but we handle these things routinely. There's no need to panic over a few sparks. The system has safeguards in place."

Aarav gritted his teeth. He knew an issue when he saw one. "Sir, I understand, but a short circuit in NICU could be catastrophic. At least let's get an electrician to inspect it."

Mr. Sharma's expression hardened. "Doctor, we have procedures. You're an intern. Stick to your department, and let us handle the technical aspects."

The dismissal stung, but Aarav didn't push further. He had learned from Dr. Nair that forcing change without understanding the politics of the system often led to resistance. Still, he left the conversation frustrated.

Two days later, at 3 AM, a sudden power outage struck the NICU. The emergency backup generators kicked in immediately, but the brief disruption caused panic among the staff. The temperature in the incubators fluctuated, and alarms blared as doctors and nurses rushed to stabilize the infants. Fortunately, no lives were lost, but the scare was enough to trigger an internal investigation.

By morning, Dr. Nair was in a meeting with the hospital board. Aarav sat outside her office, waiting anxiously. When she finally stepped out, her eyes met his knowingly.

"You reported this issue two days ago, didn't you?" she asked.

Aarav nodded. "Yes. But no one took it seriously."

Dr. Nair sighed. "That's the challenge of administration, Aarav. You can see the problem, but convincing people to act on it is a different battle."

He clenched his fists. "But this could've been prevented! If only they had listened…"

She placed a hand on his shoulder. "The problem isn't just seeing the issue—it's knowing how to present it in a way that ensures action. You need to learn when to push and when to persuade."

Aarav frowned. "How do I do that?"

Dr. Nair leaned against the desk; arms crossed. "First, you need allies. If maintenance won't listen to you, you get a senior doctor or administrator to back you up. People respect hierarchy. Secondly, data matters. If you had recorded previous incidents of flickering lights, you could've used evidence instead of opinion. And lastly, never let frustration cloud your judgment. Losing your temper or acting too aggressively will make people resist you more."

Aarav exhaled slowly, absorbing her words. He had approached the problem head-on without strategizing. Perhaps there was a better way.

Later that evening, the hospital board issued a directive for a full electrical safety audit. Mr. Sharma, now under scrutiny, personally oversaw the repairs. Dr. Nair's influence ensured the issue was properly addressed, but Aarav learned a valuable lesson—being right wasn't enough; knowing how to get others to listen was just as important.

That night, as he walked out of the hospital, he realized that his journey in hospital administration had truly begun. He wasn't just a dentist anymore—he was slowly becoming a leader.

6: Trial by Fire

Aarav's mind was made up. The more he immersed himself in the intricacies of hospital administration, the clearer his path became. But outside the walls of the hospital, he was met with resistance.

His parents were baffled. His father, a respected surgeon, saw his son's deviation from clinical practice as a waste of his years of dental training. "You studied to be a dentist, Aarav. Not a hospital manager," he argued one evening at dinner. "You should be perfecting your craft, not worrying about hospital logistics."

His friends, too, were indifferent at best and dismissive at worst. "Bro, you're literally a doctor. Why do you want to become an administrator?" one of his batchmates teased. "Isn't that what MBAs do?"

Aarav found himself defending his decision constantly. He felt like an outsider, torn between two worlds, neither fully accepting him. But before he could dwell on his struggles, a phone call changed everything.

It was the night of Diwali. The city was alive with fireworks, laughter, and celebrations. Aarav had just returned home when his phone rang. It was Dr. Nair.

"Aarav, I need you at the hospital. Now." Her voice was strained, almost frantic.

"What happened?" he asked, heart pounding.

"There's a fire in the NICU."

Aarav froze. "What?"

"The electrical panel—you were right. Something short-circuited, and the insulation caught fire. We've evacuated most of the babies, but we're short-staffed. Many senior doctors are out of town because of the festival."

"I'm coming," he said, grabbing his keys and rushing out the door.

When he reached the hospital, the sight before him was chaos. Smoke billowed from the NICU's entrance, and the fire alarms blared. Firefighters were already inside, trying to contain the flames. Nurses were rushing with oxygen tanks, transferring fragile newborns to safer areas. Parents stood outside in distress, some crying, others praying.

Aarav ran toward Dr. Nair, who was directing the staff with a strained but determined expression. "What do you need me to do?" he asked.

"Help with the patient transfers. We need to get all infants to the paediatric ICU, but we have limited incubators. Prioritize the most critical cases," she instructed.

Without hesitation, Aarav moved into action. He helped move tiny, fragile babies, monitoring their oxygen levels and ensuring they remained stable. The tension was suffocating, but amidst the chaos, he felt something else – the purpose. This was more than clinical work. This was the very soul of hospital operations—managing a crisis, ensuring patients' safety, and leading under pressure.

Hours later, when the fire was finally put out and the last baby safely transferred, Aarav collapsed onto a chair, exhausted. Dr. Nair sat beside him.

"You handled that well," she said, giving him a tired but proud smile.

Aarav swallowed, his throat tight. "This is what I want to do, Dr. Nair. Not just dentistry. I want to heal the system. Make sure things like this never happen again."

That night, for the first time, he faced his parents—not as a confused intern, but as someone who had found his calling. With tears in his eyes, he told them, "I want to bring change to the way hospitals are run."

And this time, they listened.

7: The Path Forward *(Part 1)*

The fire in the NICU had changed something in Aarav forever. What he had witnessed wasn't just a disaster—it was a symptom of a larger illness that no stethoscope could detect. It was structural, systemic, and deeply entrenched. And he was no longer willing to treat symptoms. He wanted to cure the disease.

The morning after the fire, Aarav sat by the hospital courtyard, his scrubs still faintly smelling of smoke. He hadn't slept. But his exhaustion was overpowered by clarity.

For the first time in months, he opened his laptop not to study a dental case, but to search for courses in healthcare administration. One search led to another. One tab became ten. Then twenty. He was awash in a sea of possibilities—Master's in Hospital Administration (MHA), MBA in Healthcare Management, MPH with a health systems track, even executive programs offered by global universities.

The question wasn't just what to choose—it was *how to choose*.

Dr. Nair found him there during her morning rounds. "Did you get any rest?"

He looked up, smiling faintly. "I couldn't. Too much on my mind."

She sat beside him, glancing at his screen. "Looking at MHA programs?"

"I want to study this formally," he said. "I want to understand how hospitals function—how decisions are made, how systems are built. Not just react to problems. I want to learn how to prevent them."

Dr. Nair's smile was approving but tempered with experience. "It's not just about degrees, Aarav. It's about mindset. But yes, the right training will help you get to the table where those decisions are made."

They spent the next hour going through universities, curriculum comparisons, alumni networks, and entrance requirements. Dr. Nair told him about her own decision to switch from clinical to administrative work—how lonely it had been, how misunderstood she had felt, and how long it took to earn respect in a space where everyone expected her to be a doctor, not a strategist.

"But it's worth it," she said quietly. "When you change even one process that saves lives, it's worth it."

That night, Aarav excitedly shared his plans in the intern mess. But the reception was colder than he expected.

"So, you're *really* leaving dentistry?" said Harsh, his closest friend from college. "After all these years?"

"I'm not leaving it," Aarav explained. "I'm just... taking it in a different direction."

"Come on, man. You were the best among us in practicals. You could open your own clinic tomorrow and have a waiting line out the door," said Shruti, a prosthodontics intern.

Aarav smiled politely, but something in their tone stung. "I don't want to run a clinic. I want to run a hospital."

"You sound like an MBA," Harsh muttered.

The group chuckled, but Aarav didn't. The words lingered with him. Not because they were wrong—but because they were said to mock.

The gap between him and his peers began to widen with each passing week. While they prepared for MDS entrance exams, discussed implant techniques, or debated over case studies, Aarav was buried in SOPs, eligibility criteria for global fellowships, policy research, and webinars on healthcare economics.

He started skipping group dinners. His phone buzzed less with jokes and more with program deadlines and campus info sessions. One by one, his friendships began to wither—not out of bitterness, but simply out of lost common ground.

It was a lonely kind of clarity. But it was also liberating.

The growing silence from Aarav's friends was something he hadn't prepared for. He had always believed that ambition, if rooted in good intentions, would be celebrated. But ambition that didn't align with expectation? That was another story.

Dr. Nair noticed the subtle shifts. Aarav's cheerful energy had quieted into a deep, thoughtful stillness. He asked sharper questions now. He observed more. But the loneliness, though unspoken, hung around him like a second shadow.

One afternoon, after a gruelling hospital audit, Dr. Nair called him into her office.

"You're not sleeping well," she said as she closed her laptop.

Aarav didn't deny it. "I'm trying to figure out which course... which country... which entrance exam. There are deadlines coming up. I'm also trying to build my statement of purpose. And—" he stopped, hesitating. "And it's getting harder to talk to people around me."

She leaned back in her chair. "Because they don't understand?"

He nodded.

"I went through the same thing," she said softly. "I had a friend in med school who stopped talking to me once I said I wanted to go into admin. She said, 'You're running away from patients.' I wasn't. I just wanted to help all of them, not just one at a time."

Aarav's eyes lit up. "That's exactly how I feel."

She smiled. "Then let's talk about the next step."

Dr. Nair rolled over her chair to a side cabinet and pulled out a thick folder—marked with tabs and labeled with names of universities. "I keep this updated for students like you. Few and far between—but when they appear, I want to be ready."

Inside were handouts from IIMs offering MBA in Hospital Management, international programs like Harvard's MPH in Global Health Systems, John Hopkins' MHA, ISB's Healthcare Leadership program, and even lesser-known but powerful certifications from WHO, Stanford Online, and INSEAD's executive modules.

"The big question," she said, tapping the folder, "is not just what you want to study, but *where* you want to make an impact. Do you want to work in policy? In a private hospital chain? In government health systems? NGO health outreach? Each of these will push you toward a different kind of program."

Aarav was stunned by the scope.

"I don't know yet," he said honestly.

"That's okay," she replied. "But you'll have to start deciding soon. Some of these schools have deadlines in the next sixty days."

The following days became a blur of research.

Aarav divided his time between hospital duties, internship documentation, and late-night research sprints. He joined forums, emailed alumni, read course syllabi line by line.

He filled notebooks with comparisons—cost, duration, curriculum, post-grad pathways.

He discovered that MHA programs in India were focused, affordable, and practical. But global programs—though expensive—offered cutting-edge curriculum, international exposure, and access to large healthcare networks.

The biggest challenge? His statement of purpose.

Every time he opened a blank document to begin writing it, he felt a weight pressing on his chest. How do you compress everything—his journey, his dreams, his fire-night experience, his lonely resolve—into a few hundred words?

Dr. Nair helped him there too.

She made him do something unusual: write a *letter to his future hospital*.

"Write to the hospital you'll one day run. Tell it what kind of place you want it to be. What values it will uphold. How it will be different. Don't worry about structure. Just write."

It took Aarav four hours. But when he finished, he had something he didn't expect—tears in his eyes.

It read:

"To *my future hospital,*

You will not just be a place of treatment. You will be a place of dignity, of order, of preparedness. No patient will be turned away because of paper. No mother will have to wait for an oxygen tank. No nurse will be ignored when she raises a red flag. You will not just run—you will breathe, because your system will have a soul. I won't just be your director. I'll be your custodian."

That letter became the core of his SOP.

8: The Path Forward *(Part 2)*

Around this time, Aarav's relationship with his parents took another turn.

Although they had softened after the fire incident, they still struggled to understand the full picture.

"You want to study again?" his mother asked one morning, eyebrows furrowed.

"Yes. I want to apply for MHA or healthcare-focused MBA programs. Either in India or abroad."

His father folded the newspaper slowly. "You'll be starting from scratch."

"I'll be investing in building the skills I need to make the kind of change I want."

His father's tone wasn't angry, but it was tired. "You've spent so many years learning how to treat patients. Don't you think this is running away from your talent?"

Aarav stood silent for a while. Then he said, "Do you know what I saw the night of the NICU fire?"

Both parents looked at him, alarmed.

"I saw a nurse carrying a 1.2 kg baby through smoke, because the evacuation plan was printed and stored in a folder no one could find. I saw the emergency oxygen outlet fail because no one had maintained it. I saw panic in the eyes of parents who trusted us with their children. And I realized—our system is brilliant on paper but broken in practice. I don't want to be another person who says, 'This isn't my job.' I want to be the one who makes sure *everyone's* job is clear, safe, and respected."

His mother reached for his hand. She didn't say anything. But she didn't pull away either.

By the third week of research and application prep, Aarav had narrowed his list to four programs:

1. **TISS (Tata Institute of Social Sciences)** – for its legacy in public health systems.

2. **ISB's Healthcare Management Fellowship** – for leadership in private healthcare delivery.

3. **IIM Bangalore's Hospital and Health Management Programme** – for structure and scalability.

4. **Johns Hopkins Bloomberg School of Public Health (MPH with systems focus)** – for a global perspective.

Dr. Nair, when she saw his final list, nodded with approval. "That's a solid spread. One domestic legacy institute, one international powerhouse, one leadership-focused MBA, and one public-private interface. You're thinking like a strategist already."

What followed was a phase Aarav hadn't prepared for: the waiting game.

He had submitted two applications and had interviews lined up. But the time in between brought out a restlessness in him. His hospital internship was nearing its final months. Most of his batchmates had locked in MDS coaching plans or job offers. Some were discussing PG housing.

He was still in limbo.

One evening, he bumped into Harsh again at the hospital canteen. It was awkward.

"Hey," Aarav greeted him.

Harsh looked up from his thali. "Hey. Long time."

They sat in silence for a few moments before Aarav asked, "So how's your NEET PG prep going?"

Harsh nodded. "Final mock next week. Results in two months."

Aarav hesitated. "I'm applying for healthcare admin programs. Trying to get into Johns Hopkins, TISS, maybe ISB."

Harsh didn't respond immediately. He took another bite and then said, "You know… I made fun of you back then. But after the NICU incident, I realized you're probably doing something most of us never even thought about."

Aarav blinked, surprised. "That means a lot."

"You're still weird for liking Excel sheets and hospital layouts," Harsh teased.

They both laughed. Something softened. Maybe not complete reconciliation, but mutual respect had returned.

A week later, Aarav received his first email of acceptance—from TISS.

He stared at the screen for a long minute, not knowing whether to scream, cry, or run down the hallway. Instead, he walked straight to Dr. Nair's office, knocked, and when she looked up, he simply held out his phone.

She read the mail, then looked up at him with quiet pride. "Congratulations, Aarav."

"I… I didn't think they'd respond this fast."

"Sometimes," she said, "when you're on the right path, the road opens early."

But the true test came the following night.

His father sat on the living room sofa, watching a news debate about hospital corruption. Aarav waited until the commercial break.

"I got in," he said, voice steady. "TISS. Healthcare administration."

His father turned slowly. "That's impressive."

Aarav took a deep breath. "I know you always wanted me to open a clinic. And I respect that. But I truly believe my purpose lies elsewhere."

There was a long pause.

Then his father asked, "You remember when you were 10, and you sat beside me during my night shift in surgery?"

Aarav smiled faintly. "I was too short for the scrub table."

His father chuckled. "That night, when you saw how one call from the hospital could change everything, I thought, 'He'll make a great doctor.' I think now… maybe I misunderstood what kind of doctor you'd be."

Aarav's eyes welled up.

"Go fix the system, beta," his father said softly. "It needs people like you."

9: The Selection

It had been almost a month since Aarav submitted his applications, and by now, he had become a professional at refreshing inboxes. Every morning began with checking email. Every night ended the same way.

His first offer—TISS—had given him confidence. A week later, he cleared the written test for ISB and was scheduled for a final interview. The Zoom call was brief but intense.

They asked him about the NICU fire. About the emotional toll. About his career switch. And most unexpectedly—about leadership.

"What does leadership mean to you in a healthcare setting?" one panelist asked.

Aarav paused.

"It means being the one who stays calm when oxygen runs out. Who doesn't scream but reallocates. Who sees patients in numbers but never forgets they're people. It means being invisible when things go right and fiercely accountable when they go wrong."

There was silence. Then a slight nod from the lead interviewer.

He knew he had struck the right chord.

The acceptance from ISB arrived the following Friday. It was official. He now had two strong options—one in policy, one in leadership.

The third email came two days later—from Johns Hopkins. A regretful rejection.

Aarav wasn't crushed. In fact, he felt at peace.

Dr. Nair congratulated him again when she heard. "Now you have a choice. The hard kind. Between two rights."

Aarav took a week to decide.

TISS was legacy, powerful in policy circles, socially driven.

ISB was sharp, modern, and connected to India's evolving healthcare delivery ecosystem.

Ultimately, Aarav chose ISB. He wanted to be inside the hospitals. Redesigning the systems. Rebuilding the spine of healthcare, not just advising it from outside.

With his admission secured, he requested a quiet week off clinical duty.

Not for celebration. For closure.

He spent his days shadowing the biomedical team, the sanitation supervisor, the night shift staff nurse, even the cafeteria vendor. He asked questions about everything—from oxygen refill cycles to linen management to software updates. He took notes not as a curious intern, but as a future administrator.

On his final evening, he went to the NICU one last time.

The repairs had been completed. New wiring. Fire extinguishers on every wall. Evacuation route maps laminated and posted. A framed certificate of compliance from the city fire department.

But more than anything, what caught Aarav's eye was a tiny label stuck on the new electric panel.

"Rechecked: Feb 2 – Per Fire Audit. Flagged by Dr. Aarav Mehta"

He stood there, hand on the wall, quietly moved.

He had left a mark. Not a big one. But a real one.

That night, Dr. Nair called him into her office for a final coffee.

"You did well," she said. "And you'll do more. Just promise me one thing."

"Anything."

"Don't become a paper pusher. Don't let the bureaucracy drown your instincts. You felt something when that panel sparked. You moved people when the NICU caught fire. You're not here just to manage. You're here to protect."

Aarav nodded, the weight of her words settling on his shoulders like a quiet oath.

"I'll remember," he said.

10: Indian School of Business (ISB)

The gates of the Indian School of Business stood tall and clean, gleaming in the early morning light like a promise waiting to be fulfilled. Aarav stood before them with two bags slung over his shoulders and a flutter in his chest he couldn't suppress. These gates weren't just the entrance to a prestigious institution—they were the passage to a future he had chosen for himself, a future where he wasn't bound to a dental chair, but where he could redesign the foundation of healthcare itself.

From the moment he stepped onto campus, the atmosphere was different. The conversations in the corridors weren't about clinical cases or patient complaints—they were about policy bottlenecks, digital transformation, resource allocation, and ROI on healthcare investments. People here spoke in frameworks, strategies, and impact models. Aarav knew he was in unfamiliar territory.

His first class, "Introduction to Healthcare Strategy," was a jolt.

"You are not here to learn how to treat patients," the professor said, a former CEO of one of India's largest hospital chains. "You're here to learn how to ensure *everyone* in the hospital can do their job better—faster, safer, and smarter. You're not healing people. You're healing the system."

That sentence didn't just land. It echoed.

Aarav's heart raced. This was it. This was what he had been looking for—not just the vocabulary, but the vision.

But reality hit quickly. The syllabus was brutal. Hospital finance spreadsheets. Public health economics. Business strategy simulations. Policy deep-dives. Excel models with hundreds of rows. Dashboard visualizations. KPIs. ROI curves.

He struggled in the beginning. Not with the concepts—he understood systems. But with the pace. His classmates included IIT engineers, former consultants, public health officers, and data analysts. Most of them had a strong grasp of analytics and corporate frameworks. Aarav had empathy, instincts, and hospital floor stories. But his PowerPoint formatting? Weak. His Excel pivot tables? Embarrassing.

One night, after being called out in a group presentation for messy slides, he went back to his room and stared at his laptop until 2 a.m. refining every chart.

"This is not dentistry," he muttered to himself. "But it's going to save more lives."

Gradually, he found his rhythm. And with it, his confidence.

He started speaking up more in class. When a professor asked, "What would you do to reduce OPD wait times in a tier-2 city hospital?" he shared a real story of how one bottleneck in registration had led to cascading delays in three departments. When someone questioned the role of frontline staff in digital transformation, he spoke about a nurse in his hospital who handwrote all patient notes because no one had taught her the software.

His insights were lived, not theoretical. And slowly, people started noticing.

His classmates, initially skeptical of his clinical background, began seeking his input. During a group assignment on emergency preparedness, Aarav created a flowchart based on real hospital evacuation drills. One of the group members, Niyati—an MPH from Canada—was stunned.

"You actually ran a NICU evacuation?" she asked, eyes wide.

"I didn't run it," Aarav said, modestly. "But I helped. It changed me."

The respect in her eyes was unmistakable.

More collaborations followed. He was chosen as a team lead for a project on hospital redesign. His unique combination of empathy and operational thinking made him a natural mediator—between clinical priorities and administrative needs, between policy and implementation.

But the best compliment came during a hallway encounter with a professor who had been particularly tough on him.

"You remind me of someone," he said. "She was also a doctor who wanted to redesign the system. Her name was Aditi Nair."

Aarav's heart swelled.

Despite the wins, there were moments of self-doubt. Moments when Aarav missed the certainty of a clinical procedure, the immediacy of fixing a patient's pain. Here, everything was slow. Strategic. Sometimes intangible.

One day, during a seminar on hospital budgeting, a case was presented about a public hospital that refused to invest in backup generators due to cost. Aarav couldn't stay silent.

"We can't think of backup as an *extra*. In a hospital, it's as essential as oxygen. I've seen what happens when systems fail. You can't account for human life in budget cells."

The room fell silent. The professor nodded solemnly. "That's exactly why we need leaders like you."

One weekend, Aarav received an email from Dr. Nair.

Subject: Miss your questions

Body: "You'd be proud—we implemented your flow-based triage map in the ER. Door-to-doctor time dropped by 30%. Coffee when you're back?"

Aarav smiled. He hadn't just moved on—he had left a legacy behind.

Toward the end of the first semester, the cohort was assigned a real-world challenge: partner with a nearby mid-sized hospital and audit one operational problem. Aarav's team was given outpatient workflow.

While others focused on queues and software lag, Aarav did what few thought of—he spoke to the patients.

In the hospital lobby, he met an elderly man waiting since 7 a.m. for a follow-up. When asked why he didn't book online, the man smiled sadly. "My son works in Dubai. I just show up. I don't know how to use a smartphone."

That line stuck with him.

Aarav included a patient empathy matrix in their report. They recommended not just tech upgrades, but physical navigators—trained volunteers to guide walk-in patients through the system. Human touch in a digital flow.

Their team won best project. The hospital CEO called it "one of the most balanced recommendations we've seen—tech with soul."

For Aarav, it was validation that he could lead with compassion and still deliver outcomes.

As the semester came to an end, Aarav stood on the campus terrace watching the sun dip behind the stone lecture halls. A breeze lifted his collar, and he thought about where he had started: a confused dental intern watching admin meetings from afar. A boy torn between parental expectations and inner callings. A friend slowly distanced from his group.

Now, he stood as a leader in the making.

He opened his journal and wrote one new line below the letter to his future hospital:

"I am no longer torn. I am aligned. The system may be broken. But I am not. And I will spend my life making sure others don't break inside it either."

And with that, Aarav turned back toward his dorm—not to rest, but to build what came next.

11: The Final Term

Aarav's final term at ISB began with a quiet pressure that all graduating students knew but few spoke about—what comes next? The campus was buzzing with placement talks, corporate visits, internships, and proposals for capstone projects. For Aarav, however, the placement season was more than just about securing a role. It was about choosing the first step in a lifetime of systemic change.

He wasn't looking for a glamorous title. He didn't want to manage only budgets. He wanted his hands in the soil of operations, fixing roots.

Dr. Nair had once told him, "Find a place that's broken enough to need you, but still willing to try."

That advice guided him through the offers that came his way—some promising titles like 'Healthcare Strategy Associate' at corporate hospital chains, others offering analyst roles at consulting firms. But one opportunity stood out: a role as Operations Associate at a not-for-profit hospital in rural Gujarat that served over 800 patients daily and had just received funding to digitize its systems.

It wasn't the highest paying job.

It wasn't in a big city.

It didn't come with a title that turned heads.

But it felt right.

He took it.

His last few weeks at ISB were a blur of final presentations, capstone submissions, and late-night farewells. The friendships he had built—though different from the ones back in dental school—were genuine and rooted in mutual growth. He had found people who understood what he was fighting for.

On the night before convocation, Aarav sat again on the terrace, the same place he had stood at the end of his first semester. This time, he wasn't reflecting. He was ready.

He texted Dr. Nair: "Graduating tomorrow. I took the Gujarat role. You were right. It's broken. But they're willing."

She replied within seconds: "Proud. Now go fix it."

The not-for-profit hospital was a world away from the polished floors of corporate healthcare. It was dusty, overburdened, but filled with resilience.

In his first week, Aarav walked the premises every day, talking to every department—pharmacy, registration, lab, even the ambulance drivers. He made notes, not judgments.

He discovered that:

The patient queue system was manual.

The lab results were printed but often misplaced.

The medicine inventory was being tracked on paper.

Doctors were working 12-hour shifts with no structured feedback or review systems.

On Day 10, he held his first townhall with the staff.

"I'm not here to inspect you," he said. "I'm here to understand you. Then build with you."

That disarmed them.

He introduced a digital appointment scheduling prototype within a month. The wait time dropped by 22%.

He digitized medicine tracking using simple barcode labels.

He launched a basic patient feedback form—printed in the local language—with checkboxes for clarity.

Every time someone told him, "That's not how we've done it," he replied, "But can we try?"

And slowly, things began to shift.

Three months into the role, the hospital director—a 62-year-old physician who had built the hospital from scratch—invited Aarav to his home for tea.

"You remind me of a younger me," the director said. "Restless. Idealistic. I had that once."

"What happened to it?" Aarav asked gently.

"Life," the man said. "Budget cuts. Political interference. Staff quitting. But if someone like you had come to help me back then... maybe I'd have been less tired today."

Aarav understood. Change wasn't just about systems. It was about people. About healing their fatigue, not just fixing their forms.

One rainy evening, Aarav received a voice note from Harsh, his old friend from dental school.

"Hey, bro. So… we implemented your patient navigator idea in our new clinic. Hired a retired teacher to help elderly patients with the OPD app. It's been amazing. Also… I think I finally get why you chose this path."

Aarav smiled, tears in his eyes. Some bridges, when mended, are stronger than before.

Six months in, Aarav had redesigned three hospital workflows, reduced medication errors by 40%, launched a mobile-friendly OPD queue app, and built a new emergency response protocol using just a whiteboard and laminated cards.

But more importantly, he had restored belief.

Doctors who had once been sceptical now referred to him by name during morning briefings.

Nurses who used to ignore him now pulled him aside to report broken equipment.

And patients—the ones who didn't even know what an "admin guy" did—smiled when he walked by.

Because now, things worked.

At the end of one year, the hospital invited Dr. Nair as chief guest for their annual review.

Aarav stood beside her, giving a presentation on "Operational Efficiency in Low-Resource Settings."

When he finished, she whispered, "You didn't just learn the system. You've started rewriting it."

And as the hall applauded, Aarav's eyes found one face in the crowd—a mother holding her baby outside the NICU, safe and calm.

And that, he knew, was his real report card.

12: Foundations of a New Era *(Part 1)*

The second year in Aarav's healthcare journey didn't begin with fanfare. It began with a spreadsheet.

The operations review from the past twelve months lay open on his desk—columns and rows full of metrics: turnaround times, patient satisfaction indices, medicine stock efficiency, bed occupancy rates, incident logs. What had once seemed like intimidating data now read like a living pulse to Aarav. Every number told a story, and every outlier was a warning.

But this year was different. This year, he wasn't just fixing broken systems. He was leading a transformation.

In recognition of his work, Aarav had been promoted to **Deputy Operations Lead** at the hospital. It wasn't a ceremonial title. It meant real responsibility, real targets—and real resistance.

The hospital was preparing for its first expansion in nearly a decade: the addition of a new outpatient wing and the digitization of patient health records across all departments. A mammoth project for a modest rural institution, and Aarav had been asked to co-lead it.

"Be ready," Dr. Sharma, the hospital director, warned him. "This won't be like last year. Now you're asking people to change what they've always done."

The expansion project began with meetings.

Meetings with architects, engineers, medical officers, and most crucially—the legacy staff.

Nurses who had worked for 20 years with handwritten notes.

Pharmacists who had memorized medicine stocks by shelf color.

Clerks who feared technology like it was a disease.

Aarav started with listening.

At one of the early stakeholder sessions, he asked each department to express their biggest fears about going digital.

The radiology technician said, "If the system fails, patients will wait longer."

The head nurse said, "We don't want to be blamed when software errors happen."

The billing officer said, "What if I press the wrong button and delete someone's bill?"

Aarav took notes on a whiteboard.

Then he said, "What if this helps reduce your night shifts? What if you can spend more time treating and less time documenting? What if patients stop yelling because they don't have to wait three hours for discharge?"

He paused.

"I'm not asking you to trust the tech. I'm asking you to trust me to teach you how to use it, and to stand with you if it fails."

That turned the room.

Three months into the project, the outpatient wing construction was on schedule. Aarav worked late into the evenings with the civil engineers, sometimes sketching layout flowcharts with chalk on temporary site walls. He pushed for wide corridors, directional signage, a breastfeeding room, and designated queue bays—all inspired by the frustrations he had observed as a dental intern years ago.

His proudest moment came when he convinced the board to install a solar-powered standby grid to back up critical areas—an idea born from the NICU fire that had once changed the course of his life.

As construction on the outpatient wing advanced, the other half of the project—digital integration—lagged behind. The staff hesitated to adapt, and Aarav could feel the weight of their reluctance pressing into each corridor conversation.

What began as passive disinterest slowly morphed into resistance.

The legacy nurses called the new system a "distraction." The pharmacy team frequently defaulted to manual ledgers "just to be safe." The IT technician was young but undertrained, and system bugs—though minor—often led to panic among the older staff.

Then, it happened.

On a Monday morning, just after the hospital hit peak footfall, the newly digitized registration system froze. A server issue. Aarav wasn't on-site at the time; he was in a policy discussion in town. His phone exploded with calls.

By the time he reached the hospital, chaos had bloomed.

The outpatient waiting area was overflowing. Staff reverted to writing names on paper, but confusion over time slots caused disputes. Some patients walked out. A few shouted at the guards. One elderly man fainted from the heat while waiting.

Aarav stood still for a moment in the middle of the disorder. He watched. He listened.

Then he acted.

He went desk by desk, assigning handwritten ticket numbers while simultaneously coordinating with the IT technician to restore the system. He took the mic in the waiting hall and explained the issue in the local dialect, assuring everyone they would be seen. He personally walked three elderly patients to shade and gave them water.

By 1 PM, the system was back online.

By 2 PM, Aarav was sitting in Dr. Sharma's office, being questioned.

"Some of the staff think we're pushing this too fast," Dr. Sharma said. "They say you're changing too much, too soon."

"I understand their fear," Aarav replied. "But if we don't build this now, we'll keep going in circles."

There was a long pause. Then the director looked at him, not with anger, but with concern.

"You'll need allies, Aarav. More than just ideas."

That night, Aarav couldn't sleep. The failure—the frustration—felt heavier than it should. But before self-doubt could take over, an unexpected email lit up his screen.

Subject: Conference Speaker Invite – National Forum on Rural Health Innovation

Body: *Dear Dr. Aarav Mehta,*

We are pleased to invite you as a featured speaker for our session on "Operational Innovations in Low-Resource Settings." We believe your leadership at Shakti Rural Hospital is a case study in scalable, compassionate reform. Kindly confirm your availability...

Aarav read it twice.

A speaking opportunity. National. Public. And then, he saw the co-panelist list.

Dr.Harsh Rajput – Director, Smiles First Multispecialty Dental Group.

His oldest friend. His almost-lost friend.

The conference hall in Delhi was pristine and polished—very different from the dust and clamor of Aarav's hospital. As he walked in with his notes, a voice behind him stopped him mid-step.

"Aarav Mehta, the admin guy."

He turned and smiled.

Harsh looked older, sharper in a navy blazer, but the grin was the same.

"Didn't think I'd see you on *this* side of the healthcare table," Harsh said.

"You and me both," Aarav chuckled.

They hugged—awkward at first, then honest.

Over coffee, they spoke about everything—the NICU fire, Aarav's new role, Harsh's dental chain expansion, and the strange path that had brought both of them full circle.

Harsh shook his head at one point. "You remember how much we teased you?"

Aarav nodded. "Yeah. You were right to question me. I was questioning myself back then."

"And now?"

"Now," Aarav said, "I build hospitals that won't burn. And systems that won't break under pressure."

Harsh raised his cup. "To building the future."

13: Foundations of a New Era *(Part 2)*

The stage lights were bright, but Aarav didn't blink. He stood at the podium, the slide behind him frozen on a photograph of the Shakti Rural Hospital's OPD queue—the one that had once stretched into the street.

The moderator introduced him:

"Up next, we have Dr. Aarav Mehta, Deputy Operations Lead at Shakti Rural Hospital, who has spent the last year transforming one of India's busiest rural hospitals through human-centered design and system-level reform. His talk: *'System Is Soul: The Case for Compassionate Operations.'"*

There was polite applause as he stepped forward.

He paused for a moment, taking in the audience—administrators, doctors, policymakers, NGO reps, industry executives. People who, on paper, could make things happen. And yet, Aarav knew most hadn't stepped into a rural OPD in years.

He started with a story.

"In February last year, a woman walked into our hospital carrying her child. She had traveled 43 kilometers in a shared jeep, waited five hours to register, and when she finally saw the doctor, we realized she had been sent to the wrong department. Her frustration wasn't about the illness. It was about being invisible in the system."

He clicked to the next slide—his team's OPD flow redesign with empathy markers.

"Our goal wasn't to be digital. It was to be *visible*. We added human navigators before we added tablets. We introduced bilingual signage before we introduced apps."

He then walked them through hard numbers:

- 32% reduction in wait times

- 40% reduction in medicine errors

- A 60% increase in positive patient feedback on clarity and comfort

But it wasn't the metrics that made the room go still.

It was the moment he looked up and said, "A healthcare system isn't just bricks and billing. It's the sum of every ignored suggestion, every overworked nurse, every file that goes missing. We say healthcare is broken. I say we've forgotten to look at it like a *human body*. You don't fix a failing heart with better packaging. You need care from within."

A slow silence. Then thunderous applause.

After the session, Aarav was mobbed. Representatives from NGOs, hospital chains, even state health departments asked for his slides, his notes, his models. One woman, a policy fellow from Bengaluru, said, "We need this mindset. Not just for one hospital—but for a hundred."

Later that evening, at the networking dinner, Harsh clinked a glass beside him.

"You stole the show."

"I told the truth," Aarav said simply.

Harsh tilted his head. "You ever think of building this bigger?"

Aarav looked at him. "Every day."

That night, he didn't sleep. He sketched instead—on a hotel notepad—the first vision of something new: **A scalable hospital operations mentorship model.** A project that could coach rural hospitals on building their own compassionate systems, starting from within.

He would call it:

Project Hridayam.

Heart.

Because even hospitals needed one.

14: Project Hridayam

The next morning, Aarav boarded his return flight with no suitcase—just a notepad filled with scribbles, flowcharts, and what he'd started calling "compassion logistics." Where some people packed souvenirs, he packed visions.

Back at Shakti Rural Hospital, things were running smoothly. The outpatient wing was nearing completion, and the digital transition—once rocky—was becoming routine. Staff who had resisted Aarav now invited him for chai, and some even brought him patient cases they felt the system could serve better.

But Aarav was no longer satisfied with just one hospital. Something had shifted at the conference. He had seen what it meant to speak at scale—to influence not just patients and colleagues, but policies and mindsets.

He scheduled a meeting with Dr. Sharma and laid out his idea.

"Sir, I want to launch an initiative—a mentorship model for low-resource hospitals to help them redesign systems with local empathy and limited cost."

Dr. Sharma leaned forward. "You want to export Shakti's model?"

"No," Aarav said. "I want to co-create others. Each hospital will have different needs. We just guide them with what we've learned and build with them."

The director didn't answer for a long moment. Then he smiled. "What will you call it?"

"Project Hridayam."

He nodded. "You'll need a team. Time. Funding."

"I'll find it," Aarav said.

And so, Project Hridayam began—quietly at first.

Aarav reached out to every hospital contact he'd made in the last two years. Small facilities in UP, NGOs in Rajasthan, a district hospital in Assam, a rural women's health center in Maharashtra. He sent them each a one-page proposal and an invitation.

Within a month, he had five confirmations.

By month three, he had ten.

He designed the model like a health mentorship program:

- **Stage 1: Listening Visits** – A small team would visit the hospital and interview staff from every department.

- **Stage 2: Shadow Mapping** – Following the journey of patients through the hospital to identify bottlenecks.

- **Stage 3: Co-Design Clinics** – Workshops with staff to brainstorm low-cost, locally sourced system improvements.

- **Stage 4: Pilot and Review** – Implementing one major change and reviewing results within 60 days.

- **Stage 5: Peer Sharing** – Hosting mini-forums for hospitals to share progress and learn from each other.

It wasn't perfect. It wasn't fast.

But it worked.

The pilot hospitals reported small but powerful changes:

- One reduced maternal wait time in OPD by introducing queue tokens run by village volunteers.

- Another introduced color-coded patient folders that helped non-literate caregivers navigate departments.

- One hospital, inspired by Aarav's own story, instituted fire safety drills and labeled their panels, proudly writing: "Audited by Hridayam Team."

Aarav traveled constantly—on dusty trains, through stormy roads, into villages with no cell signal. He carried a bag of forms, a toolkit of printed guides, and a portable projector. But what he gave most generously was **hope**.

He listened. Not as a savior, but as a partner.

One evening, after a long training session in a community clinic in Bihar, a young nurse stopped him.

"Sir," she said, "we don't have many machines here. But now, because of that new flowchart, patients wait less. It feels less... noisy."

Aarav smiled. "That's what systems are supposed to do. Make care feel calm."

She looked down and added, "I feel calmer, too."

That night, Aarav added a new line to his journal.

"When systems work, humans breathe better."

By the end of the year, Project Hridayam had supported **17 hospitals**. Aarav had built a small core team of five—

two nurses, one health designer, a public health fellow, and an operations intern. They weren't bound by titles. Only by mission.

His journey was no longer a detour from dentistry. It was a destination he had carved through fire, doubt, and faith.

And as he stood once again in front of a new hospital team, drawing another patient map on a whiteboard, he realized something:

He wasn't just healing hospitals anymore.

He was helping hospitals learn to **heal themselves**.

Epilogue – The Architect of Healing

Years had passed since Aarav Mehta first walked into the hospital as an intern—young, idealistic, and conflicted. Back then, he had held a scaler in one hand and confusion in the other. He was a promising dental student, praised for his clinical precision, but burdened by a question that refused to fade: *Is healing only about treatment, or could it be something more?*

Now, standing at the head of the National Health Infrastructure Reform Council, Aarav's journey had come full circle—only this time, he wasn't entering a hospital to shadow. He was entering to lead.

The room was packed with delegates from over 20 states. Behind him stood a team of health architects, policy planners, systems engineers, and operational experts. Before him was a screen that read:

"Project Hridayam: 5-Year Impact Review – Healing the System, Hospital by Hospital."

Aarav's voice echoed through the grand conference room.

"Five years ago, we set out not to revolutionize healthcare with expensive machines or billion-dollar buildings—but to give dignity to the smallest clinics, the ones where systems were paper, power outages were common, and yet care never stopped."

He clicked to the first slide: a tiny rural hospital in Bihar, now restructured, digitally enabled, and featuring a community-run patient support kiosk.

"In 47 hospitals, we didn't just reduce patient wait time—we restored trust. In 20 clinics, we didn't just digitize records—we made them understandable to the people who mattered most: patients and their families."

His voice softened.

"And in every place, we visited, we asked the same question—not 'What's wrong?' but 'What could work better, if you had a chance to try?'"

The hall erupted in applause. But for Aarav, applause was never the goal. He stepped down from the stage and let his team take over the Q&A. His joy wasn't in headlines, but in hallway whispers: the stories of tired nurses who finally got time to rest, or anxious patients who left with clarity instead of confusion.

Outside the venue, Aarav sat quietly in the garden, sipping black tea. The sky had turned gold. He opened his phone and scrolled through his photo gallery—images of before-

and-after hospital entrances, cluttered registries turned into clean dashboards, chalk-scrawled walls now lined with laminated flowcharts.

But his fingers paused on an old photo.

It was the NICU panel—the spark that had started it all. A photo taken on a panicked night. In the corner was his hastily scrawled note: *"Reported—risk not addressed."*

That moment had never left him. It had burned itself into his story—not as trauma, but as transformation.

Aarav's home office told a story too.

On one wall hung a whiteboard with sketches from his latest pilot—an AI-supported triage assistant for resource-scarce clinics. On another wall were framed memories: a smiling photo of his Shakti Rural Hospital team after the OPD launch, a thank-you letter from the TISS faculty who had once reviewed his SOP, and a worn-out print of the fire safety evacuation plan.

But perhaps the most precious item sat on his shelf: his first journal.

Dog-eared, coffee-stained, and fragile, it held his journey in scribbles. Thoughts jotted down between patient rounds, strategies built late into the night, quotes from mentors, and one simple promise:

"I don't just want to be good at dentistry. I want to be great at care."

He flipped to the last page. There, he had written something new a few months ago:

"Healing isn't only what we give. It's what we build so others can give it too."

The next morning, Aarav visited Shakti Rural Hospital.

It was tradition. Every year on the anniversary of the NICU fire, he returned—not as a director, not for a press event, but as someone paying respect.

He greeted the old staff, some of whom were still there, older now, greyer. He saw the new interns, young and nervous, unaware of the legacy that lived in those walls. He walked the halls, touched the new electric panel—modern, fireproof, labeled in three languages—and smiled.

Then, as always, he went to the NICU.

The cribs were clean. The monitors blinked steady. The room was calm.

He stood quietly near the door until a nurse noticed him.

"Dr. Aarav?" she said.

He nodded.

"We have your checklist laminated at the station," she smiled. "And your story... they tell it to every new hire."

He smiled back; eyes moist.

When he left, he took the long route out. Through the corridor where he once questioned a faulty record. Past the room where Dr. Nair had first spoken to him. Down the staircase he had rushed through that night, holding a file, holding purpose.

In the car ride back, Aarav called his parents.

"Maa, Baba," he said, "Shakti looks beautiful. I wish you could see it."

"We're already proud, beta," his mother replied. "But we'd still love to visit."

His father added, "Maybe next time, you can show me the panel you fixed."

Aarav chuckled. "It's not about what I fixed, Baba. It's about what we built after that."

Later that week, Aarav received an invitation to join the National Health Systems Reform Board. It was a position of influence, of change—but also of politics and pressure.

He thought about it for a while. Then, before answering, he asked for one condition: "Let me take my team from Hridayam with me. I won't work without the people who believe in ground-up design."

They agreed.

That evening, Aarav sat on his porch, journal in hand. The wind rustled the pages.

He thought back to the day he had confessed his dreams to his parents. To the day Dr. Nair gave him a folder of programs. To the day he watched a system fail and decided to become the kind of person who would never let it fail again.

He flipped to the front of the journal and wrote on the inside cover:

"For the dreamers who don't wear capes—but carry clipboards. The healers who don't hold stethoscopes—but hold the line. May we always remember: care begins long before the scalpel. It begins in systems that breathe."

And with that, he closed the book.

His story wasn't ending.

It was simply evolving.